W9-CHZ-184

IMAGINITIVE

Trains

A Level One Reader

By Cynthia Klingel and Robert B. Noyed

The Child's World®

All aboard! Here comes the train.

Trains carry many things.

Some trains carry coal.

Some trains carry wood.

City trains carry lots
of people.

Some people ride trains to work.

13

Some trains go under the street.

Some trains go above
the street.

Trains move on tracks.

It is fun to ride a train.

Word List

city

coal

street

tracks

wood

Note to Parents and Educators

Welcome to The Wonders of Reading™! These books provide text at three different levels for beginning readers to practice and strengthen their reading skills. Additionally, the use of nonfiction text provides readers the valuable opportunity to *read to learn*, not just to learn to read.

These leveled readers allow children to choose books at their level of reading confidence and performance. Level One books offer beginning readers simple language, word choice, and sentence structure as well as a word list. Level Two books feature slightly more difficult vocabulary, longer sentences, and longer total text. In the back of each Level Two book are an index and a list of books and Web sites for finding out more information. Level Three books continue to extend word choice and length of text. In the back of each Level Three book are a glossary, an index, and a list of books and Web sites for further research.

State and national standards in reading and language arts emphasize using nonfiction at all levels of reading development. The Wonders of Reading™ fill the historical void in nonfiction material for the primary grade readers with the additional benefit of a leveled text.

About the Authors

Cindy Klingel has worked as a high school English teacher and an elementary teacher. She is currently the curriculum director for a Minnesota school district. Writing children's books is another way for her to continue her passion for sharing the written word with children. Cindy Klingel is a frequent visitor to the children's section of bookstores and enjoys spending time with her many friends, family, and two daughters.

Bob Noyed started his career as a newspaper reporter. Since then, he has worked in communications and public relations for more than fourteen years for a Minnesota school district. He enjoys writing books for children and finds that it brings a different feeling of challenge and accomplishment from other writing projects. He is an avid reader who also enjoys music, theater, traveling, and spending time with his wife, son, and daughter.

Published by The Child's World®, Inc.
PO Box 326
Chanhassen, MN 55317-0326
800-599-READ
www.childsworld.com

Photo Credits
© Bruce Hands/Tony Stone Images: 9
© Christopher Arneson/Tony Stone Images: 18
© Cosmo Condina/Tony Stone Images: 14
© 1996 Dusty Perin/Dembinsky Photo Assoc. Inc.: cover
© Glen Allison/Tony Stone Images: 10
© Helberg/Unicorn Stock Photos: 6
© JeffGreenberg@juno.com/Unicorn Stock Photos: 13
© 1999 Michael P. Gadomski/Dembinsky Photo Assoc. Inc.: 5
© Michael Townsend/Tony Stone Images: 17
© Photri, Inc.: 21
© Vic Bider/PhotoEdit: 2

Project Coordination: Editorial Directions, Inc.
Photo Research: Alice K. Flanagan

Copyright © 2001 by The Child's World®, Inc.
All rights reserved. No part of this book may be
reproduced or utilized in any form or by any means
without written permission from the publisher.
Printed in the United States of America.

Library of Congress Cataloging-in-Publication Data
Klingel, Cynthia Fitterer.
Trains / by Cynthia Klingel and Robert B. Noyed.
p. cm. — (Wonder books)
Summary: Illustrations and simple text describe different kinds of trains and the work they do.
ISBN 1-56766-810-0 (lib. reinforced : acid-free paper)
1. Railroads—Trains—Juvenile literature.   [1. Railroads—Trains.]
I. Noyed, Robert B.   II. Title.   III. Wonder books (Chanhassen, Minn.)

TF148 .K55   2000
385—dc21   99-057450